PREHISTORIC
Scary Creatures

Franklin Watts®
An Imprint of Scholastic Inc.
NEW YORK • TORONTO • LONDON • AUCKLAND • SYDNEY
MEXICO CITY • NEW DELHI • HONG KONG
DANBURY, CONNECTICUT

Written by
John Malam

Created and designed
by David Salariya

Author:

John Malam studied ancient history and archeology at the University of Birmingham, England. After that he worked as an archeologist at the Ironbridge Gorge Museum in Shropshire. He is now an author specializing in nonfiction books for children on a wide range of subjects. He lives in Cheshire, England, with his wife and their two young children. Website: www.johnmalam.co.uk

Artists:

John Francis

Carolyn Scrace

Mark Peppé

Catherine Constable

Nick Hewetson

Jackie Harland

Series Creator:

David Salariya was born in Dundee, Scotland. He established The Salariya Book Company in 1989. He has illustrated a wide range of books and has created many new series for publishers in the UK and overseas. He lives in Brighton, England, with his wife, illustrator Shirley Willis, and their son.

Editor: Stephen Haynes

Editorial Assistants:
Rob Walker, Tanya Kant

Picture Research:
Mark Bergin, Carolyn Scrace

Photo Credits:
iStockphoto

PAPER FROM
SUSTAINABLE
FORESTS

Megatherium

Created, designed, and produced by
The Salariya Book Company Ltd
25 Marlborough Place, Brighton BN1 1UB

A CIP catalog record for this title is available from the Library of Congress.

ISBN-13: 978-0-531-21747-4 (Lib. Bdg.)
978-0-531-21901-0 (Pbk.)
ISBN-10: 0-531-21747-7 (Lib. Bdg.)
0-531-21901-1 (Pbk.)

Published in 2009 in the United States by
Franklin Watts
An Imprint of Scholastic Inc.
557 Broadway
New York, NY 10012

Printed in China

Contents

Ambulocetus

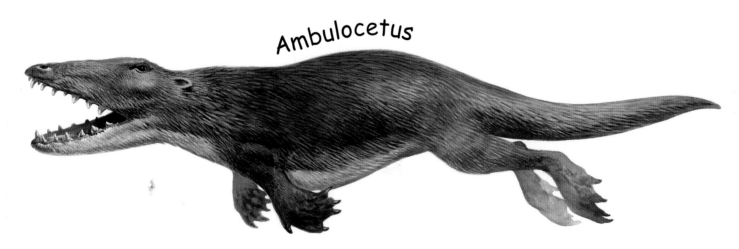

What Was the Biggest Land Mammal?

Long ago, Earth was ruled by **reptiles**. Dinosaurs walked the land, **pterosaurs** were masters of the sky, and **plesiosaurs** swam the seas. About 65 million years ago, most reptiles died out. This book is about the new group of **prehistoric** animals that took over. Many were **mammals**. The biggest land mammal was Indricotherium.

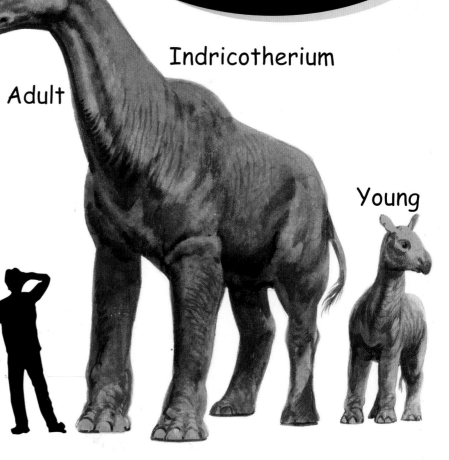

X-Ray Vision

Hold the next page up to the light to see inside an Indricotherium.

See what's inside

Indricotherium

Adult

Young

How big was it?

A fully grown adult Indricotherium was about 18 feet (5.5 m) tall, 26 feet (8 m) long, and weighed 20 tons (18 metric tons). Indricotherium lived in Asia. It became **extinct** about 25 million years ago.

No people were alive 25 million years ago. The little figures of people in this book are just to give you an idea of how big the prehistoric animals were.

Indricotherium was an **herbivore**. It ate plants and could strip leaves from the tops of trees.

Long neck

Large top lip

Three toes on each foot

5

Its skull was 4.2 feet (1.3 m) long.

Hollow bones in its back and neck helped to reduce weight.

Indricotherium is an extinct mammal. Its closest living relative today is the rhinoceros.

Modern rhinoceros

Why Were Prehistoric Rhinos Woolly?

Coelodonta was a woolly rhino with a coat of thick fur. It lived in Europe and Asia between 50,000 and 10,000 years ago, during an **ice age**. Its woolly coat kept it warm in the cold climate.

How long were its horns?

Coelodonta had two horns. The front horn was up to 3 feet (1 m) long. The back horn was shorter. Elasmotherium, the largest of the prehistoric rhinos, had a single horn about 6.5 feet (2 m) long.

Did You Know?

Coelodonta was hunted for its meat by early humans known as Neanderthals. Their stone tools of sharp **flint** cut the rhino's body into chunks.

Elasmotherium

Coelodonta

What Was the Biggest Shark?

Dorsal (back) fin

Megalodon

Backward-pointing teeth

Gill slits

Pectoral (chest) fin

Imagine a shark twice as long as a present-day great white shark, with a mouth 6.5 feet (2 m) wide. This was Megalodon, a super-sized dolphin-eater, 52 feet (16 m) long. It was the biggest shark ever. Megalodon was the ocean's **top predator**, the supreme hunter of its time. It could attack and eat other animals, and no other animals attacked it. It became extinct about 1.6 million years ago.

How big were its teeth?

Megalodon had as many as 250 teeth. Some were 8 inches (21 cm) long. When it bit its **prey**, some teeth might snap off—but new ones soon grew in their place.

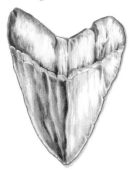

Megalodon tooth

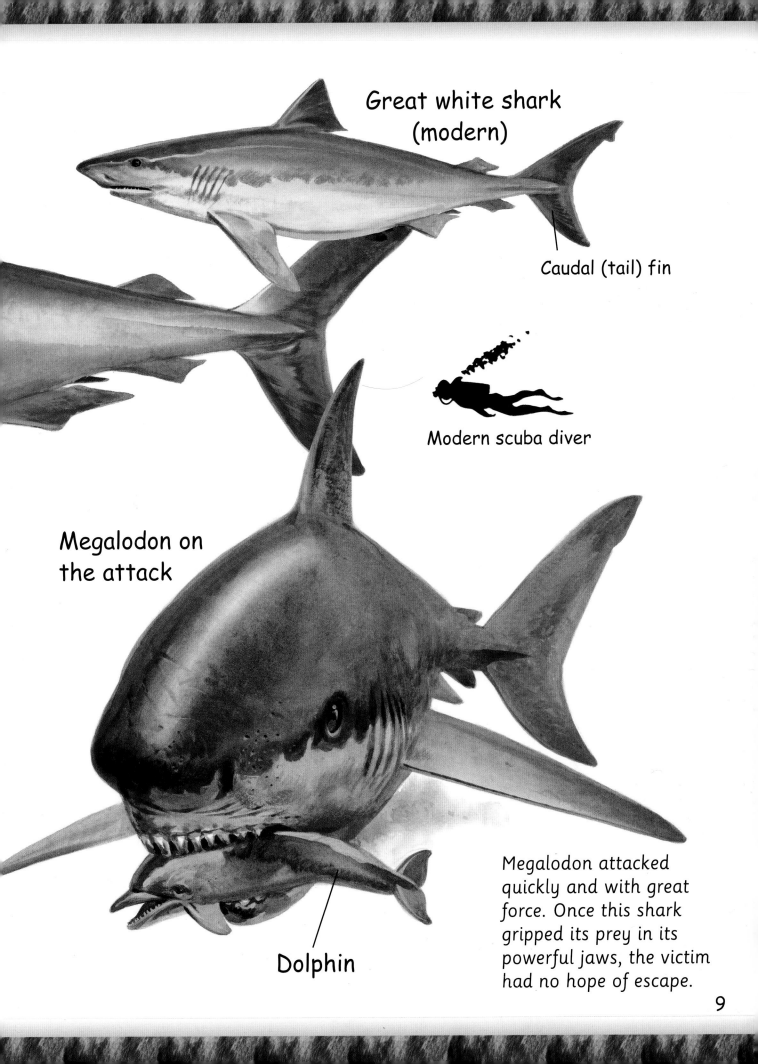

Great white shark
(modern)

Caudal (tail) fin

Modern scuba diver

Megalodon on
the attack

Dolphin

Megalodon attacked
quickly and with great
force. Once this shark
gripped its prey in its
powerful jaws, the victim
had no hope of escape.

What Were "Terror Birds"?

Terror birds were the scariest birds ever. These huge beasts, all now extinct, had tiny wings and could not fly. They were meat-eating hunters that stalked forests and swamps, looking for mammals to **ambush** and eat.

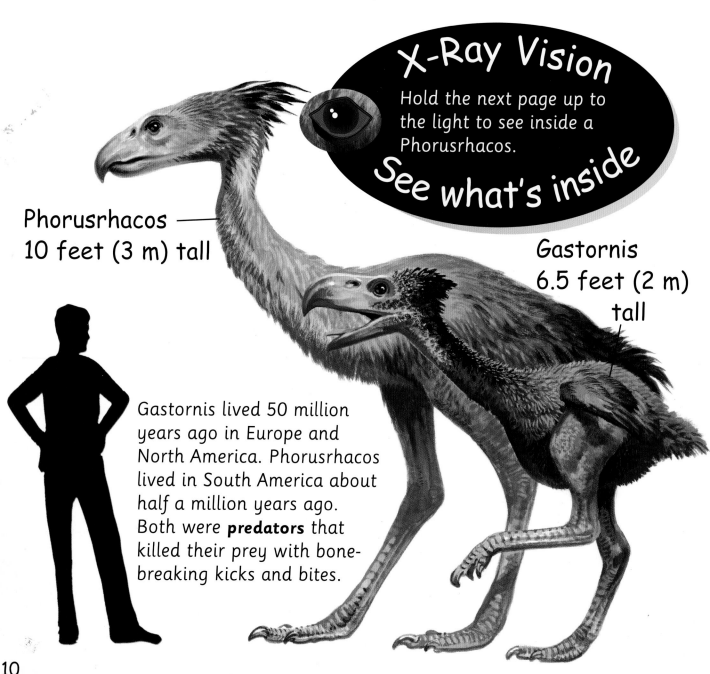

X-Ray Vision

Hold the next page up to the light to see inside a Phorusrhacos.

See what's inside

Phorusrhacos
10 feet (3 m) tall

Gastornis
6.5 feet (2 m)
tall

Gastornis lived 50 million years ago in Europe and North America. Phorusrhacos lived in South America about half a million years ago. Both were **predators** that killed their prey with bone-breaking kicks and bites.

Phorusrhacos

A Smilodon cub has been taken by a hungry Phorusrhacos. The bird's kicks will be enough to keep the cub's parent away.

Smilodon cub

Powerful legs

Clawed toes

Smilodon

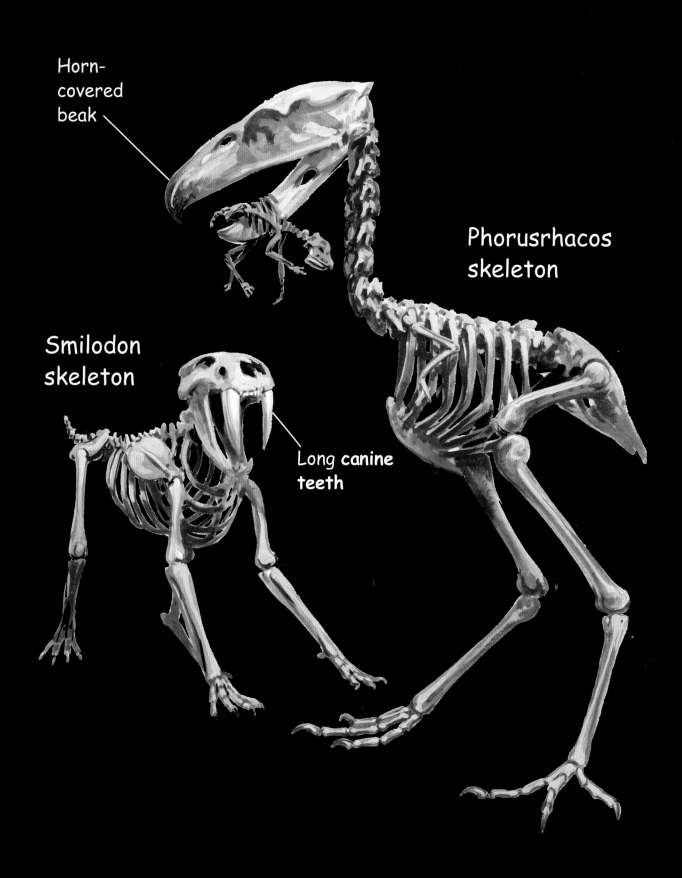

Horn-
covered
beak

Phorusrhacos
skeleton

Smilodon
skeleton

Long **canine**
teeth

Why Did Some Cats Have Big Teeth?

Smilodon was a **saber-toothed** big cat. The **canines** (pointed teeth) in its top jaw were up to 8 inches (20 cm) long and were curved. Smilodon probably used them to deliver a killing bite to its prey.

Smilodon lived in North America and South America. It first appeared about two million years ago. It became extinct about 10,000 years ago.

What did Smilodon eat?

Smilodon preyed on large mammals such as bison, mammoths, deer, and bears. It dragged them to the ground and ripped open their soft, fleshy sides.

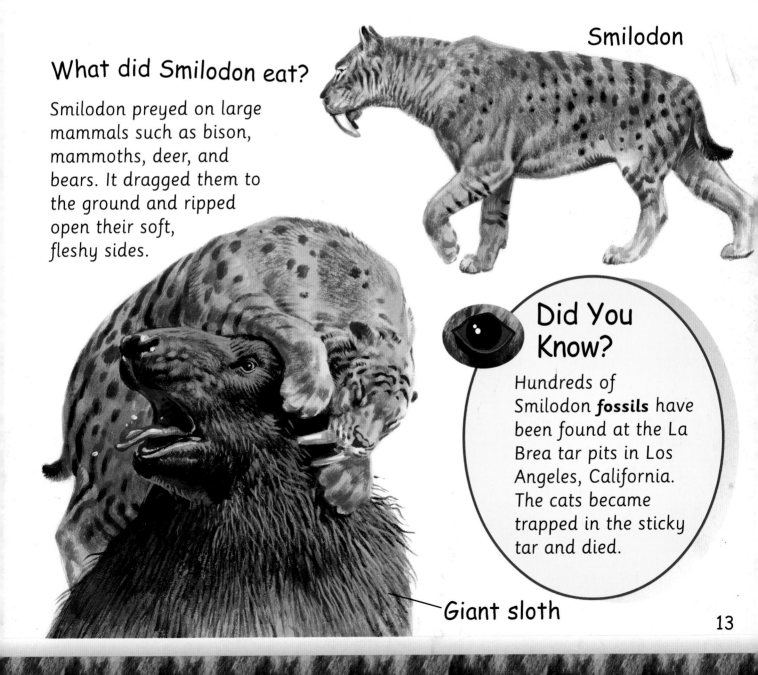

Smilodon

Did You Know?

Hundreds of Smilodon **fossils** have been found at the La Brea tar pits in Los Angeles, California. The cats became trapped in the sticky tar and died.

Giant sloth

13

Why Did Mammoths Have Hairy Coats?

Woolly mammoths lived 50,000 years ago, when Earth's northern regions were in the grip of an ice age. **Glaciers**—huge masses of ice—covered large parts of Europe and North America, and animals that lived in these areas had adapted to the cold. The woolly mammoth's thick fur kept its huge body warm.

High, domed head

Did You Know?

A mammoth's tusks were actually its front (**incisor**) teeth which had become incredibly long. The longest woolly mammoth tusk ever found is 13.5 feet (4.1 m) long!

Woolly mammoth

African elephant

How big was a woolly mammoth?

A fully grown woolly mammoth was about the same size as an African elephant—10 feet (3 m) tall and weighing up to 5.5 tons (5 metric tons).

Long, curved tusks

Small ears

Sloping back

What Mammals Lived in the Sea?

Pointed teeth

Flipper feet with long toes

Ambulocetus was one of the first sea mammals. It was an **ancestor** of the whale, but it didn't look anything like the whales we know today. It lived in Asia, and could walk on land and swim in the sea. A meat-eating predator, it lay in wait to ambush passing prey. It became extinct about 50 million years ago.

Ambulocetus was the size of a big sea lion.

Ambulocetus was 10 feet (3 m) long.

Long, thin tail—not a tail **fluke** like today's whales have

Did You Know?

Ambulocetus had ears inside its skull, connected to its jaw. By resting its jaw on the ground, it sensed vibrations from nearby animals.

What did it eat?

Ambulocetus lay in wait for passing mammals, such as this primitive horse. It ambushed them and dragged them into the water, where they drowned.

Were There Sloths as Big as Elephants?

Megatherium was a giant ground sloth that lived in South America. It was as big as a modern elephant. It lived in grassy areas and was a herbivore, eating leaves and other vegetation. It became extinct about 8,000 years ago.

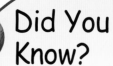

Did You Know?

Fossil footprints 3.2 feet (1 m) long and 16 inches (40 cm) wide have been found preserved in mud. They show that Megatherium could walk upright on its two hind legs.

Why so big?

Megatherium became a monster-sized animal for two reasons. There was plenty of food for it to eat, and it had very few enemies. There was nothing to stop it from growing to a huge size.

Megatherium weighed 5 tons (4.5 metric tons).

How did it eat?

Megatherium could reach leaves at the tops of trees by standing up on its hind legs and using its tail for support. It probably hooked branches with the three long claws on its fingers, and then stripped the leaves off with its peglike teeth.

Thick fur

Short,
heavy tail

Clawed
fingers

What Was the Biggest Carnivore?

The biggest meat-eating land mammal that ever lived was Andrewsarchus. This **carnivore** was not a hunter, but a **scavenger** that ate **carrion**. It may have found food by sniffing for rotting flesh, just as the modern hyena does. Also like the hyena, Andrewsarchus probably ate whole **carcasses**— flesh, hair, skin, and bones. It died out 35 million years ago.

How big was Andrewsarchus?

A fully grown Andrewsarchus was about 16.4 feet (5 m) long and more than 6.6 feet (2 m) tall. Its massive head was 3 feet (1 m) long, and its jaws were packed with sharp teeth.

Andrewsarchus

Andrewsarchus lived in present-day Mongolia, in eastern Asia. Its sharp front teeth were adapted for tearing at flesh, and its flatter back teeth could crunch and crush bone.

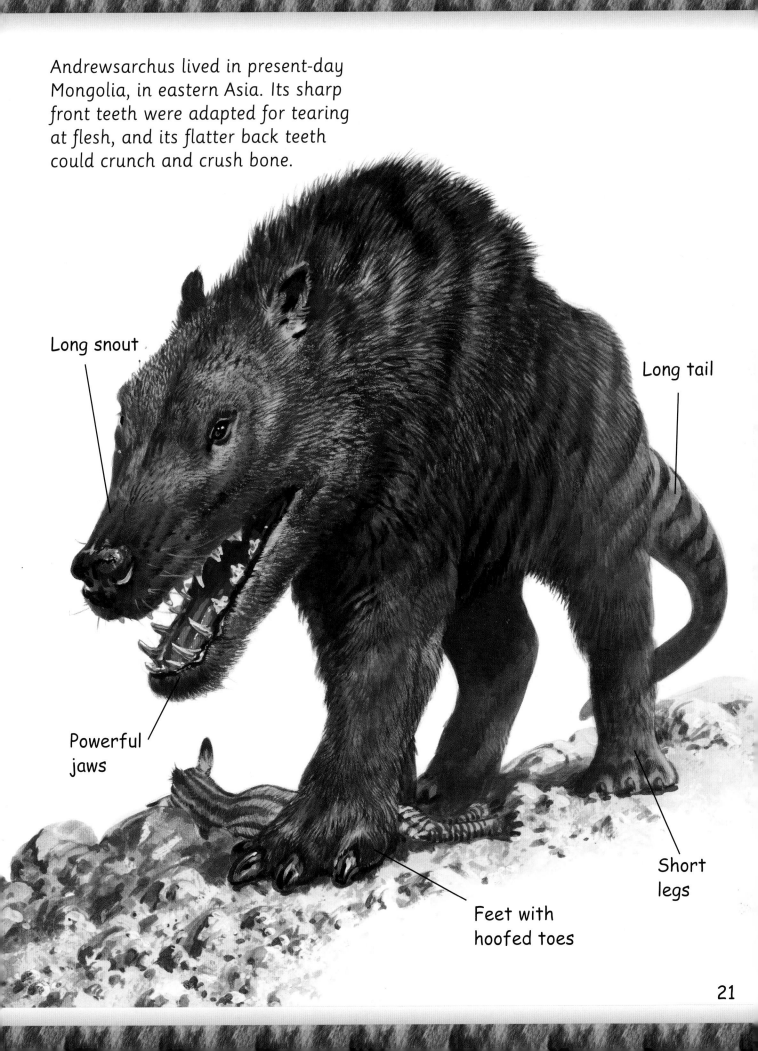

Long snout

Long tail

Powerful jaws

Feet with hoofed toes

Short legs

Basilosaurus

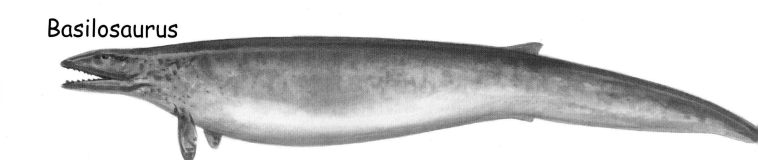

Did Sea Serpents Ever Exist?

Tail fluke

Long,
slender body

No, but Basilosaurus is
one of the closest things to
a sea serpent that has ever
existed. One of the world's
first whales, it had a very
long, snakelike body and a
small head. To swim, it moved
its tail up and down,
"beating" the water with its
tail fluke. Basilosaurus became
extinct 35 million years ago.

Basilosaurus was 69 feet
(21 m) long.

Durodon

Did You Know?

Basilosaurus breathed air, as whales do today. But, unlike modern whales, it did not have a **blowhole**. To breathe, it came to the surface and breathed air through its nosrils.

Long jaws packed with teeth for biting and slicing

What did Basilosaurus eat?

Basilosaurus was a carnivore. As it swam in the world's oceans, it hunted fish, squid, sharks, turtles, and smaller whales. Unlike modern whales, it could not dive deeply. It killed its prey quickly with powerful jaws that clamped around the victim. Sharp, pointed teeth in the front of the whale's jaws pierced the prey's body. Then, saw-edged teeth in the back of its mouth cut the prey into pieces, ready to be swallowed.

Who Are Our Ancestors?

About four million years ago, a new kind of animal appeared in Africa. It was a slender creature that walked upright on two legs. It was Australopithecus, a human ancestor. As time passed, Australopithecus **evolved** into other human ancestors. Eventually, modern humans came along.

Early tools

Axes, scrapers, and other early tools were made from flint.

Australopithecus (Southern Ape). Died out around 3 million years ago.

Homo habilis (Handy Man). Died out around 1.8 million years ago.

Homo erectus (Upright Man). Died out around 500,000 years ago.

Homo sapiens (Wise Human). Modern humans appeared 200,000 years ago.

How did people survive during the ice ages?

Building a mammoth-bone hut

Warm clothes made from skins and furs

Modern humans first moved to Europe about 60,000 years ago. By 20,000 years ago, when much of Europe was covered in glaciers, humans had made the region their home. They had to learn how to survive in an ice age.

Our ancestors lived by hunting for mammoths, deer, and bison. They also gathered berries, roots, and other plants. Caves and overhanging rocks gave them shelters to live in, and some groups made huts.

Completed hut

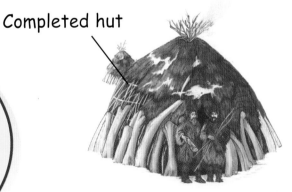

Did You Know?

Sea levels were lower during the ice ages than they are today. A land bridge joined northeastern Asia to North America, and people and other animals could walk between the continents.

Ice-age **hunter-gatherers** in eastern Europe made huts from woolly mammoth bones and tusks. They were the world's first handmade structures.

Why Did Mammoths Die Out?

Around 20,000 years ago, mammoths roamed across Europe, Asia, and North America. By 10,000 years ago they were more or less extinct. Why? Mammoths died out because as the ice age ended and the climate warmed up, their **habitat** disappeared and they could not survive in a changing world. Hunting by humans also reduced their numbers, until there were none left at all.

Did You Know?

The very last mammoths died out only 4,000 years ago. They lived on Wrangel Island in the Arctic Ocean, and they were tiny—only about 3 feet (1 m) tall.

Early humans hunting a mammoth with weapons of wood and stone

How did ice-age hunters trap and kill mammoths?

Mammoths were hunted for their meat, fur, and ivory. Hunters may have dug pits for the mammoths to stumble into as they walked by. They may also have forced them over cliffs. The great beasts were killed with wooden spears that had sharp stone tips.

Pit disguised with branches

On the Island of Jersey in the English Channel, the bones of 20 mammoths have been found at the bottom of a ravine. It's thought that the mammoths were chased over a cliff to their deaths. Their skulls were smashed open, possibly so the hunters could get at the animals' tasty brains!

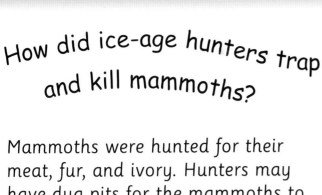

Ice-age hunter-gatherers trapping a mammoth

How Do We Know About Prehistoric Animals?

Scientists have found the fossilized bones of prehistoric animals all over the world. Many of these fossils are just individual bones, but sometimes a complete skeleton is found. When this happens, the animal can be reconstructed so we can see what it looked like when it was alive, thousands or millions of years ago.

Fossilized skeleton of a woolly mammoth

Where are fossils found?

Most fossils are found in **sedimentary** rocks, such as limestone and sandstone. Long ago these rocks were just small sediment (specks of loose rock) carried along by water. As time passed, the sediment turned into solid rock and preserved the remains of animals trapped within it.

Finding a fossil

1. A fossil leg bone is discovered.

2. The bone is protected with **resin**.

3. The surrounding rock is cleared.

4. The bone is covered in plaster.

5. The bone is carefully removed.

After a fossil has been dug up, it is taken to a laboratory. The plaster covering is taken off, and the last bits of stone are carefully removed. The bone is then prepared for mounting with the rest of the skeleton.

Preserved baby mammoth

It's not just bones that get preserved. Whole bodies of mammoths have been found in the icy ground of Siberia, in northern Russia. Even parts of the fur, skin, and insides are still preserved.

Prehistoric Animal Facts

Eobasileus was a chunky plant-eater that looked a bit like a bigger version of a rhinoceros. It had six short, blunt horns on its head and a pair of curved tusks. It died out 35 million years ago.

Mastodons lived at the same time as mammoths and looked similar to them, but the two animals were not closely related. Some mastodons had four tusks; some had flat tusks shaped like shovels. Mastodons ate tree leaves, while mammoths ate ground plants. Mastodons died out about 10,000 years ago.

The ancestors of the mammoth were short and could reach the ground with their mouths. As they evolved into bigger animals, their mouths got farther away from the ground, but their trunks allowed them to reach down for food.

The first horses appeared about 50 million years ago. They were tiny animals, such as Hyracotherium, which was just 8 inches (20 cm) high and 24 inches (60 cm) long.

Brontotherium herds roamed the open woodlands of North America. These massive herbivores stood 8 feet (2.5 m) tall. They had a long pair of blunt horns on their snouts. Fossil hunters have found hundreds of them that were killed when volcanoes erupted and buried them in ash. They died out 30 million years ago.

The giant elk Megaloceros lived in Europe and Asia until about 8,000 years ago, when it became extinct. Its massive antlers measured almost 13 feet (4 m) from tip to tip.

About 3.6 million years ago, in what's now Tanzania, Africa, three Australopithecus left footprints in soft ground. The footprints became fossilized and are evidence that our early ancestors had learned to walk upright. Two of the group walked side by side and the third followed along, treading in the prints of the largest individual. Perhaps this was a family group—parents with their child.

Smilodon

Glossary

ambush To attack prey from a hiding place.

ancestor An animal from which a later animal is descended.

blowhole A breathing hole on top of a whale's head.

canine teeth Pointed teeth next to the front teeth (incisors).

carcasses Bodies of dead animals.

carnivore An animal that eats mostly meat.

carrion The decaying flesh of a dead animal.

evolve To change slowly over millions of years.

extinct No longer alive anywhere in the world.

flint A type of stone that can be broken to make tools with sharp edges or points.

fluke A whale's tail.

fossil The remains or traces of a living thing, preserved in the ground.

glacier A large mass of ice.

habitat The place where an animal naturally lives.

herbivore An animal that eats mostly plants.

hunter-gatherers Humans who travel from place to place, hunting animals and gathering plants for food.

ice age A time when Earth was cooler than today, and polar ice caps and glaciers covered much larger areas.

incisors The biting teeth at the front of the mouth.

mammal An animal that is born alive and then fed by its mother's milk.

plesiosaur An extinct marine reptile.

predator An animal that kills and eats other animals.

prehistoric Belonging to a time before the invention of writing.

prey An animal that is hunted by other animals for food.

pterosaur An extinct flying reptile.

reptile A cold-blooded animal with a backbone and with scaly skin.

resin A substance that hardens when it dries, such as fiberglass.

saber-toothed Having long canine teeth curved like a saber (sword).

scavenger An animal that feeds on carrion.

sedimentary rock A type of soft rock made from very fine particles (sediment) that settled at the bottom of rivers, lakes, and the sea.

top predator (or **apex predator**) A predator that is not preyed upon by any other animal.

Index

Andrewsarchus